Princess Asha and the Lost City of Dwarka

by

Lisa Margaret Bishop

Princess Asha and the Lost Cities

Book 1

The Lost City of Dwarka

Book 2

The Lost City of Shambhala

(Coming 2018)

Be sure to check out our Facebook page 'Princess Asha and The Lost Cities'

www.princessasha.com

For information contact

author@princessasha.com

First printed edition May 2018

ISBN: 978-1-9996020-2-4

Dedication

I dedicate this book to:

My beloved husband, Gavin Bishop, who always sees the best in me and supports me in everything that I do.

Anthony Mahabir, who has helped me with my spiritual awakening and has always believed in me.

To all of my friends and family who have supported me through this journey.

Table of Contents

Prologue

Once upon a time in an ancient city called Mathura in India, there was an evil tyrant king named Kamsa. King Kamsa was insecure and feared that the gods would kill him, so he ruled the kingdom into darkness and executed anyone that opposed him.

One day as King Kamsa was journeying on his chariot with his newly-wed sister, Devaki, and her husband, he heard a prophecy that his sister would bear a godly child that would one day destroy him. Enraged, he grabbed his sister by the hair and took his sword out to sever her head.

"You have betrayed me sister: there is a prophecy that you will one day bear a son that will destroy me," King Kamsa said angrily.

As he raised his sword, a voice came from behind,

"King Kamsa, you have nothing to fear from Devaki, she is not your nemesis," Devaki's husband said to the king.

"You love your sister, don't let this darkness in your heart do something that you will regret."

King Kamsa thought for a moment. As demonic as his soul was, he did love his sister very much.

"Very well, you will live out your lives together in the underground prison. I will control you and any children that you may have," the king said, before he ordered the guards to take them both away.

Several years passed by, and Devaki and her husband were about to have a baby. It was the middle of the night and all was quiet in the kingdom of Mathura. After hours of labor, a beautiful baby boy was born and they named him Krishna. His skin was beautiful and dark, because of his godly energy. His dark skin looked blue like the bluest of oceans. He had dark wavy hair and the biggest brown eyes. He was very, very handsome.

"We must smuggle him away before the king finds him," Devaki said to her husband. "Take him to the Yadavas so that his foster parents can protect him."

With tears in her eyes, Devaki kissed her son goodbye and watched her husband break out of the prison with baby Krishna. The escape had been planned for many years.

"Hurry back my love, before the guards notice that you are gone," Devaki cried out.

Baby Krishna was safely spirited away and Devaki's husband returned without King Kamsa suspecting anything amiss.

The years soon passed and word spread to King Kamsa that a godly child was born and was alive and well, living with foster parents. King Kamsa was furious. He called upon his demon devotees to be rid of Krishna. Unfortunately for King Kamsa, his demon devotees all failed to complete the task.

Krishna grew into a very handsome young man, with a smile that would melt your heart. He always wore a peacock's feather in his hair and carried around his favorite flute, which he would play for anyone who would listen. When Krishna played, people would say the music was so beautiful that the water would dance. Krishna was very charming and soon became a leader amongst his friends, as well as his elders. He was kind and treated everyone around him with integrity and respect.

In time, Krishna came of age to fulfil the prophecy and to destroy King Kamsa. He decided to take on his uncle once and for all. It was time to end the evil of the kingdom of Mathura. All of the Yadavas followed Krishna into a mighty battle. Once he had destroyed his uncle, they settled in Mathura until many other evil kings tried to avenge King Kamsa.

"We cannot stay here any longer, it is not safe," Krishna told his people. They all headed to safety in Gujarat on the west coast of India.

When they reached Gujarat, Krishna headed to the ocean to call upon the Lord of the Seas. He picked up his flute and started to play the most magical music. The water started to move with the sound and a giant rose from the ocean.

"My Lord," Krishna said. "I have come to ask you to please gift me some land so that I may protect my people from evil."

"I know of your good deeds, Krishna, and I will honor your request," said the Lord of the Seas. He submerged back into the ocean and a beautiful island arose.

The deities built the most magnificent city that was home to nine hundred palaces, all made of gold and jewels, where rivers and waterfalls flowed through gardens and the city center. They called this island city Dwarka and it spread for miles over the ocean. Many evil kings and their demon devotees tried to destroy Dwarka and the Yadavas, but failed every time. Krishna was so powerful that nothing was able to destroy him.

Krishna married, had a family and ruled his kingdom for many years with love and kindness; his people were all very devoted to him. He provided the Yadavas with a very rich and comfortable lifestyle; they wanted for nothing and everyone was happy.

Unfortunately, this was to change for the Yadavas. Krishna began to notice that his devotees were becoming egotistical, loving themselves above all else. Life on Dwarka was going to their heads and greed and selfishness started to take control. All of the riches offered in this mystical city were no longer enough. People were becoming angry and hostile toward one another. Krishna sat quietly and watched as his people deteriorated in front of his eyes.

The greed and selfishness didn't end in Dwarka; it spread to other kingdoms who were also fighting each other. Kings were no longer happy with their own land; they wanted to conquer other kingdoms too. These kings would come to Krishna to ask for his help in their aggression. Krishna, being the kind and loving king that he was, tried to talk the cities out of going to war. Unfortunately, they did not listen. No matter how hard he tried to bring peace and love, there was no hope. Too much anger and hatred existed in the hearts of humanity, so Krishna decided that he would no longer intervene.

More wars broke out and many people died. A queen devoted to her husband and to Krishna blamed him for not intervening. The queen believed that Krishna could have prevented the wars, but chose to stand by and watch while her sons, grandsons and husband all died.

"You did this!" the queen angrily said to Krishna as she was crying over her husband. "You could have prevented this and you chose not to," she cried out to Krishna.

In the queen's rage, she cursed Krishna, his beloved city of Dwarka and all of his devotees.

"For this, I will curse you along with your people and Dwarka. In thirty-six years, your people will turn to fury and your city will sink to the bottom of the ocean floor with all who live there," the queen said pointing at Krishna in rage.

Krishna knew that he could not make it right with the queen and that the Yadavas had become greedy and selfish. He wholeheartedly accepted the curse and his ultimate fate.

As time passed, small disputes erupted into massive fights. The curse had started to take effect and the Yadavas became very angry with one another. It started with angry words and blame and then became violent, during which Krishna was forced to take refuge in the forest.

He lay down under a tree to think of what to do next. As he was peacefully lying there, a hunter came along. He mistook Krishna for a deer and accidently shot him in the foot. The hunter was devastated that he had shot his king with his poisonous arrow. Krishna told the hunter that he forgave him, but sadly died shortly after.

Immediately waves covered the golden city, it started to sink and eventually was back at the bottom of the ocean from whence it came. Luckily, the surviving Yadavas and Pandavas were able to escape the floods.

All of the survivors gathered together and mourned Krishna, then one of the elders took control.

"We must head to the Himalayas: far away from here so the curse can no longer affect us. We will settle there and rebuild a new kingdom."

"We must forget about what has happened here in Dwarka and never speak of it again," another of the elders added.

One of the survivors was Krishna's great-grandson. When he came of age, he was crowned king of their new kingdom.

As years went by, mankind started to forget about Dwarka and the existence of the adored King Krishna. More and more families across India came to settle and build their farms in and around this beautiful new kingdom. Life became normal and the past forgotten. Nobody spoke of

Gods and Goddesses or of evil demons. These stories became fairy tales and legends.

A new chapter had begun. Unbeknownst to humans, the next chapter was Kali Yuga, the beginning of the dark ages.

There was a prophecy that was kept as a secret within one single family. It said that one day a princess, the descendant of Krishna would be born. She would be the chosen one, the pure of heart who would awaken consciousness to help bring the people of India out of the darkness of Kali.

The family protected and passed down the flute of Krishna through the generations. They taught that when this child is born, the protector of Krishna's flute will see the box that holds it, light up like the sun. When the time comes, the protector would one day pass the flute unto the chosen one.

Until then the flute must stay hidden from mankind.

Chapter 1 - The Descendent

The centuries passed and there was a new king and a new queen of the kingdom they named Panchala, located in the Himalayas. This kingdom, that was built by the remaining Yadavas and Pandavas, had become quite populous over the hundreds of years. Everybody seemed happy and adored their loving king and queen.

The queen was pregnant with her first child, a baby girl. The new princess was about to be born.

A guard ran in to tell the king. “She’s arrived, Your Majesty.”

“It’s a girl?” the king asked.

The guard grinned and nodded.

“IT’S A GIRL!” the king shouted, hugging the guard in his muscular arms.

The king excitedly ran through the palace halls to see his new daughter, the princess. When he walked into the room, there she was in her mother’s tired arms, the most beautiful baby girl he had ever seen. She had dark brown wavy hair and the biggest brown eyes; her skin was a silky pale brown.

The king took her into his arms, kissed her on her forehead, and looked at the queen with tears in his eyes.

"Princess Asha?" the king questioned as he beamed at his queen.

"I love it, it's beautiful, just like her," the queen responded.

"Princess Asha it is," the king said happily.

The whole kingdom of Panchala rejoiced and celebrated for days because there was a new royal heir.

On the same day the princess was born, away in the countryside, a humble farmer saw a very bright light beaming from underneath a stall in his barn. The light shone so brightly that it nearly blinded him. The farmer looked up at the palace, smiled and thought to himself, *this is the one, the pure of heart is here at last.*

As years went by, the princess grew into an exquisite little girl, but she started to realize that there was more outside the palace walls. Intrigued to find out, she tried to climb over the tall layer of bricks that kept her away from the marketplace and socializing with the village people. Little did the princess know, the wall wasn't there to keep her in; it was there to keep evil out. Unfortunately for her, she was still too small and not strong enough to climb over it. As she fell to the ground, scratching her arms, her royal nanny, Nisha, finally caught up with the mischievous child.

"Princess Asha, your father would have my head if he knew that you were out here climbing this wall," yelled Nisha. "Little girls do not climb, and they especially do not go looking for trouble," she angrily added, as she dragged the princess by the arm into the palace.

“This is the second bath today, miss. You need to put a leash on that girl,” the royal attendant said in frustration to Nisha as she scrubbed the dirt off the princess.

The princess looked up at her nanny and the attendant with her big brown eyes and dirt all around her face, whilst the two of them talked about her as if she wasn’t even there.

As Nisha was dressing the princess in her beautiful purple and gold sari and brushing her long wavy dark hair, the princess asked her, “Why do I feel like I don’t belong here? What is wrong with me?”

Nisha replied, “Sweetheart, there is nothing wrong with you. You are just headstrong and independent. You are so young and have so much to learn about your kingdom and the people. Be patient. You will know your destiny as you get older and wiser."

Looking at her nanny with an empty expression, the princess sat on her plush rug in her palace quarters and turned to her studies.

More years passed and soon the stunning princess was nearly sixteen. The king and queen finally allowed her to go to the farmers' market with Nisha.

"This is so exciting," the princess squealed. "I can't believe I finally get to go and see the world."

"I wouldn't really call it the world, Asha," Nisha replied as she was making Asha's bed. "It's just villagers, markets and smelly farms. I wouldn't get too excited."

The princess did not care; she had never been outside to meet the people or to see the animals before and it was going to be an adventure for her.

As they walked through the market, Nisha went off about her business purchasing fresh fruits and vegetables. The princess decided to do a little of her own poking around. She found herself in a small dark alley all alone.

“Pssst.” There was a sound from behind one of the doors.

Asha looked around, curious.

“Pssst, over here.” The voice became a little clearer.

Asha looked around and saw an old lady behind a red door calling her to come in. She walked toward the door and peeked inside.

"Come in, come in my child," the old lady called out.

As the princess walked in, she looked around the old cottage and saw stones heating under fire in metal trays and peacock feathers all over the walls. It almost looked like a witch's cauldron. Asha was very confused as to what this old lady wanted with her.

The old lady grabbed Asha's wrist, which made her jump.

"You need to fulfill your destiny, my dear. Karma will be our doom," she said quietly.

As Asha pulled her arm away from the grip of the old lady, she said, “I don’t understand what you mean.”

Before the lady could respond, Asha could hear her nanny’s voice calling for her.

“Coming!” Asha shouted.

“What are you doing in here?” Nisha cried out. “You cannot be here Asha, it is forbidden and dangerous,” she said as she grabbed Asha by the hand and pulled her away, looking over her shoulder to give the old lady an evil eye.

“Why is it dangerous and forbidden? The old lady didn’t bring any harm to me,” Asha said, angry and confused. “Who is she anyway? How does she know who I am?”

Nisha stopped, looked into Asha's eyes and said, "She is known as a witch. People believe she does witchcraft; she talks about an evil and cities that never existed. Quite frankly, I think she is just crazy, but the people here believe that she is evil. You just need to stay away from her. Oh, and everyone knows who you are — you are the princess." They continued walking back to the palace.

That night Asha couldn't sleep; all she could think about was that old lady and what she had said. *Was she just crazy?* Asha thought. *What destiny do I have to fulfill? What does she mean by karma? How can karma be our doom?* All of these questions ran through her head, even the one about the lost cities her nanny was talking about. *Are there really lost cities? Where would they be?*

Morning came quickly. The princess was ready to explore the palace library for anything that she could find about the history of India and all of its cities. As she looked at all of the books, she found one about an adoring king named Krishna and his beloved mystical city of Dwarka. Asha had never heard of this king before or his city.

"Is this just a myth or a fairytale?" she asked herself out loud.

Asha decided to take the book to her room and started reading it. As she read through the pages about gods and goddesses, kings and queens, love, wars, curses and many romantic and sinking cities, she became more intrigued. She didn't understand why no one had ever mentioned these stories to her before.

"I have to find out more," she said, slamming the book shut.

"Find out more about what?" Nisha asked as she walked in.

"Uh, find out more about what we are going to do today," Asha said with a grin as she shoved the book under her pillow.

"You are going to study while I go out to the farm to get fresh milk," Nisha sternly said.

"A farm! Oh please, can I go with you? I have never been to a farm," Asha asked with her hands clasped together, begging.

"Asha, please don't whine. Princesses don't belong on farms," Nisha replied.

"Yes, that is true, but it is good for a princess to get to know her people. To get out there and appreciate all the hard work that they do for our village," Asha said, standing up tall and confident. "I'm nearly sixteen and I want to know the people of my kingdom."

Nisha gave a deep sigh, knowing the princess was up to no good, but allowed her to come along anyway. "I honestly don't know what I'm going to do with you," she said, shaking her head. "No running off this time. Do you understand me?"

"Yes, I will only talk to the animals," Asha said with a chuckle.

They headed to a farm with hundreds of acres. There were cows, pigs, chickens and goats everywhere as well. Asha had never been to a farm, so she was amazed by everything that she saw. There was a beautiful cow with brown and light pink patches all over her body. Asha decided to go into the pastures to see this particular cow that had caught her eye.

"Hello, pretty girl, what's your name?" Asha asked, and then thought, *she can't answer you, stupid.*

"Kamada is her name," a voice said from behind.

Asha jumped in surprise, she thought that she was the only person around. She looked around to see a man in ripped-up trousers, high boots and a long-sleeved red shirt. His boots were covered in mud.

"Sorry to make you jump, Your Highness. I did not mean to scare you. My name is Aadesh. Welcome to my farm. These are my cows that provide all of the milk for the kingdom. Kamada is the oldest cow here, many of these other cows are her children."

"She is beautiful but very fat," Asha said with a bit of disgust.

"She isn't fat, she is pregnant. This is going to be her last baby before I retire her," the farmer explained. "Would you like to help me milk her?"

"Oh yes, please, I would love to help. I have never milked a cow before, so I'm not quite sure what to do," she exclaimed.

"I'm more than happy to teach you, Your Highness." The farmer grabbed Kamada by the halter to lead her into the barn.

As they walked into the barn, Asha noticed a hand-drawn painting of a handsome young man. He had long, dark wavy hair and big brown eyes; he was holding a flute. “Who is this man?” she asked, staring at the painting.

“That is Krishna. He was king of the golden city called Dwarka many, many years ago. Some even said he was a god,” Aadesh explained. “The city no longer exists. Stories have been told that there was a curse and the city was taken to the bottom of the ocean from where it came.”

“I read about this king and his city in a book. I thought it was just fairytale,” Asha said gently. “If this king did once live, and this city did truly exist, why don’t people speak of it? Why have I not learned about such a place?”

"People don't like to talk about things they fear. If they talk about it and learn about it, then they have accepted it. The truth scares people; they don't know how to deal with the knowledge. So we stop talking about it, it gets forgotten and the past no longer exists the way it truly was. Does this make sense to you?"

"I suppose so," Asha answered softly, still staring at the painting.

The painting felt real to her; she felt a bond between Krishna and herself. She felt drawn to him, as if there was much more that she had to learn about this king and his lost city.

Asha and the farmer went into the stalls to milk the cows, so she could take some back to the palace. The royal nanny came in with bottles full of milk in her arms.

"Asha, I'm ready, I have the milk," she called out.

"Me too, look, I did this myself," Asha said, excitedly running out of the stalls and spilling milk everywhere.

Nisha rolled her eyes as she put tops on the jars of milk and placed them in the basket to take back home. As they were leaving the farm, Aadesh stood at the gates waving goodbye to them with Kamada by his side.

The next morning, Asha decided to read more about this King Krishna. She felt an urge to learn more about this wonderful, mystical city and why anyone would curse it.

How could a city just fall down into the bottom of the ocean and why couldn't anyone find it? All of this boggled her mind. Asha had many questions, but no-one seemed to want to answer them.

As she sat on the steps in the courts of the kingdom, she watched her people going about their business. Asha began to wonder what these people truly thought and believed. Were they too scared to come out and talk about what they knew or had learned from their ancestors about their past? Or were they all just too scared to learn the truth?

Asha just had to learn more and the only place she felt comfortable asking her questions was at the farm. She quietly snuck around the corner of the courts, pulling her shawl over her head so that no one would recognize her as she left the Palace.

Asha got through the gates without being noticed and ran for the hills, over to the farm. Aadesh was out tending to the cows as she ran over to him, out of breath.

"My dear princess, what an honor to see you back so soon," Aadesh said. "Did you forget something?" he asked, looking confused.

"I would like to learn more about Krishna and his city of Dwarka. Would you teach me?" she asked.

"I can teach you, but it must be done without anyone knowing. Are you capable of keeping this a secret?" Aadesh responded.

"Yes sir," she shouted out excitedly.

"Sshhhh," the farmer said.

"I mean, yes sir," the princess whispered. "Can we start today?"

"Yes, I can tell you some stories today," he replied.

Days turned into weeks and weeks turned into months. The two of them got together every day to talk about the life of Krishna and his lost city of Dwarka. Aadesh would talk and Asha would listen whilst they herded and milked cows. Aadesh even taught the princess how to make butter.

There was something more to this farmer though, something he wasn't telling Asha, but she just couldn't quite figure it out.

One day as they were herding the cows, Asha decided to ask Aadesh about the witch.

“Do you know anything about the witch?” she asked. “The one in the village,” she added.

“You mean the old lady in the village, the one with all the peacock feathers?” he replied. “She isn’t a witch. She is a very old and wise woman.”

“Then why does everyone call her a witch?” asked Asha.

“That is fear my child. Remember when I said that when people don’t understand something, they fear it. They make up stories that aren’t really true to make that person look crazy. Then they start the name-calling,” Aadesh explained.

"It's getting late Asha, you should start heading home before they send the guards out looking for you. I can't even think about what your father would do to me if he knew that you were here." the farmer said grabbing hold of his neck.

Aadesh walked Asha to the gates and watched her run over the hills back to the palace.

Asha and Aadesh grew closer and closer as the months went by. It wasn't just about Dwarka anymore; Asha finally felt that there was someone who understood her, someone who would listen and answer all of the questions she had about the stories she was reading from her books. There was still a voice in the back of her mind that told her there was something more to this farmer she had become very fond of.

Chapter 2 - The Gift

It was a special day in the kingdom of Panchala. The palace bells were ringing loudly, and the royal attendants were getting ready for the royal birthday party. It was Princess Asha's sixteenth birthday and there was going to be a huge celebration to which everyone was invited.

Asha's royal nanny walked into her room singing happy birthday to the beautiful princess, but she was nowhere to be found. “Asha, Asha, where are you?” Nisha called out. “Where is that girl?” she mumbled under her breath.

Asha didn’t care about getting ready for her party; she just enjoyed spending time on the farm listening to the stories Aadesh had to tell and herding the cows. Today wasn’t just a special day for Asha: Kamada was also having her baby today.

“She isn’t due for another week,” Asha said in a panic. “We aren’t prepared for this.”

“Asha, my dear, cows have pregnancies just like we do. You can never be completely prepared for birth. It can happen any time in the last couple of weeks of pregnancy,” Aadesh replied calmly.

“Come, let’s get ready for our new arrival. We need supplies, some hot boiling water and towels.” They gathered the necessities they needed and headed over to Kamada.

It took hours of labor before the final push and the calf was finally there. It was a cute female with big brown patches all over her body and a very pink nose.

“She is adorable,” squealed the princess. “I just want to hug her, except she has goo all over her, yuck!” Asha cried out as she pulled her arms from around the calf.

The farmer couldn’t stop laughing as he watched Asha pour the remaining water from the bowl over her arms to get rid of the slime.

"What were you expecting?" he asked, still laughing. "Babies aren't born clean."

"I really didn't think about it, to be honest. This is so gross. I'm never doing this again, I'll just watch next time," she said with disgust. "We need to give her a name."

"Hmmm, why don't you name her?" Aadesh said. "She will be yours anyway, so you should name her."

"Mine? You are giving her to me?" Asha asked excitedly. "Why are you giving her to me?"

"My gift to you. It is your sixteenth birthday, correct?" Aadesh answered. "But," he continued with a sterner voice, "you cannot take her until she has been weaned from her mother."

"Oh yes, I completely understand, thank you, thank you, thank you. I can't believe I'm going to have my own pet cow. I promise I will take really good care of her and bring her back every day to visit," Asha said, hugging Aadesh.

The bells started to ring again and Aadesh and Asha both looked toward the palace. Asha knew it was time to go and be with her family and guests for her birthday. She said goodbye, pulled her shawl over her head, and headed over the hills and through the village. As she walked through the empty streets, Asha realized that everyone was at her party except for her.

There was a short cut that could get her to the palace faster, but it was getting dark and she was a little frightened to go on her own through the dark alley. The princess had no choice but to do it; it was either the creepy dark alley or be punished for the rest of her life. So, Asha took the turn into the dark alley and headed for the palace gates.

Halfway up the alley a familiar voice called to her from behind. “Asha, it is time,” the voice said. “It is time for your journey to begin.”

Asha stopped breathing for a few seconds and looked behind her. There standing next to the crooked walls of the really old buildings was the ancient peacock feather lady. Asha’s first thought was to run as fast as she could, but then she remembered what the farmer had said about her. She trusted Aadesh and if he believed the old lady wasn’t a witch but was actually wise, then Asha would believe it too. She let out a deep breath and walked over to her.

"It's time for what?" Asha questioned. "Were you talking to me?"

"It is time for you to start your journey. You are the pure one, the descendant of Krishna. It is time for you to bring love and faith back into the people, awaken consciousness back into humanity and raise Dwarka again. You are the chosen one, the one to rid us of all evil before we are all doomed for eternity. The darkness is starting to take over." the old lady said to Asha in her croaky voice, pointing her wrinkly old finger up at the princess.

Asha looked blankly at the old lady, not sure what to say or do. She looked at her with her big brown eyes and told her that she was late for her party and had to go. Stunned and confused, Asha turned around and ran as fast as she could to the palace. She ran straight into her room and shut the door, leaning up against the closed door to catch her breath. Her heart was racing.

Once she had caught her breath and calmed down, Asha went to change out of her filthy clothes and got into her best party outfit. As she shut the dressing room door behind her, she heard another familiar voice. This voice was scarier, though.

"Princess Asha, where have you been all day?" Nisha shouted. "Do you know how many excuses I have had to make to the king and queen to cover for you? You are lucky it's your birthday today, otherwise you would be on your own to answer to your parents," Nisha said, calming herself down.

"I'm so sorry, I went to the farm to help deliver the baby calf. I promise I will let you know next time," said Asha. "Please don't tell my parents," she added, batting her eyelashes.

Nisha pulled out a book from behind her back. "I also found this book under your bed. Where did you get it from? You know you aren't supposed to read this nonsense. Your parents would be so angry if they found out."

"How do you know it's nonsense? What if the stories are true? They have to come from somewhere. I don't understand why no-one will talk about our history or where we came from," shouted Asha.

“Cities don’t just disappear, Asha,” Nisha explained. “There are no such things as curses and demons. You need to promise that you will stop reading this nonsense and concentrate on your studies. Otherwise I will be forced to tell your parents.”

“We should get to my party. We don’t want to keep everyone waiting,” Asha said sadly. The two of them walked down the corridors in silence, not knowing what else to say to each other. It was an awkward moment where neither would break the silence.

As they arrived at the ballroom, there stood hundreds of people waiting to greet the young princess. Many other royal families had come from faraway kingdoms to wish the beautiful princess a happy sixteenth. They brought many gifts and even sons to introduce to Asha, hoping that maybe a small spark would ignite between the princess and their prince.

By the end of the night, Asha was exhausted. She had never danced so much in her life and with so many princes. They all wanted to win the heart of the beautiful princess, but she had no interest in any of them. Except for maybe one that is, a prince who she thought was really handsome and charming. He had dark brown hair and beautiful green eyes; he was tall and looked very strong. Asha had danced with him for most of the night, but she found it hard to keep up a conversation with the prince, as much as she tried. All she could think about was the old lady in the alley and what she had said to her.

"What journey?" Asha said, not realizing that she was thinking out loud.

"Excuse me?" the prince replied as he stopped in the middle of the ballroom.

Asha had to think of something quickly to say.

"How was your journey?" she responded, hoping that he hadn't heard her properly the first time.

"It was long, but the weather was good, so we got here faster than we thought," said the prince.

They continued to dance for a while longer, but soon Asha decided she was tired and wanted to retire for the night. The birthday princess bid the prince a good night, went to say goodnight to her parents, and left in a hurry for her room.

Nisha ran after her to find out why the princess would leave her own party so early.

“Your Highness, wait,” she called out. “Why are you running off so early?” Nisha was out of breath from running up so many steps to catch up with the princess. “I think the prince of Gujarat seemed quite smitten with you. Did you not feel the same way about him?”

“Oh yes, he was very nice and very handsome. I’m just really tired and need some rest,” Asha replied. “Would you mind thanking him for such a wonderful evening and ask him to join me in the garden for some breakfast in the morning, please?”

Nisha left, and Asha went and sat on her beautifully cushioned seat next to her large window, looking out onto the courtyard. She could see her guests slowly leaving to go back to their homes.

As Asha was watching her guests leave one by one, she couldn't get the old lady's voice out of her head. She needed to find out more.

Asha decided to get to bed so that she could get up early and go to the farm to ask Aadesh some questions. *Maybe he will be able to give me some answers,* she thought as she was laying her head on her pillow.

The next morning Asha was up and ready to walk to the farm, but she didn't want her nanny to escort her. How do I leave without her noticing? she asked herself. I could tell her I'm going to the library for more books for my studies.

As Asha walked out of her room, Nisha walked into her, knocking her study books right out of her arms. She looked at Asha, confused as to where she was going and why.

"Namaste, Princess," Nisha said. "Where are you off to so early in the morning?"

"Actually, I'm off to the library. I've finished with these books and need to get some new ones," Asha answered skeptically, not sure whether or not her nanny believed her.

Nisha stared at Asha for a couple of minutes and then remembered, "Don't you have a breakfast date with the prince this morning?"

Asha put her hand on her forehead and closed her eyes, shaking her head. "Ugh, I forgot about that. Would you mind telling him that I'm really busy studying please. I promise to make it up to him?"

"You can't keep letting people down, Your Highness. It isn't polite, especially coming from a princess," her nanny said sternly. "I will tell him only this once. The next time you can do your own dirty work."

She carried on into Asha's room to make her bed and tidy up. Asha heaved a huge sigh of relief and ran through the hallways as fast as she could. She covered her head with her shawl and went through the staff stairwell so that no one would see her leave. The princess finally left the main gates to the palace and ran as fast as she could to the farm, full of questions she wanted answered.

As Asha walked into the barn, Aadesh was sitting there waiting, as if he knew that she was coming. As she walked in, he stood up from the haystack he was sitting on, waiting for the anxious princess to speak.

"Why does the old witch lady speak to me in a strange way?" Asha asked. "As if I have some sort of special mission!" she continued before the farmer could answer the first question.

"Princess Asha, please, sit," said Aadesh, pointing to a chair next to the haystack he was sitting on. He sat back down on the hay. "You are the descendant of Krishna and you are also the chosen one. You have been chosen to fight the evil that has been destroying our world for thousands of years. It is your destiny to raise Dwarka."

Asha looked blankly at Aadesh, not quite sure whether to run, scream, or laugh at everything he had said. As she sat there, not knowing what to say, the farmer got up and walked into one of the stalls. He raked some of the hay to the side and opened a hatch. Kneeling down, he pulled out a very antique box. Aadesh took his fingers and moved them along a snake symbol. When he was done the box opened as if it was magic. He held out the box in front of the princess. As Asha gazed down inside, she was pretty unimpressed with what she saw.

"It's a flute!" she exclaimed. "What is so special about a flute?"

"This isn't just any ordinary flute, Your Highness. This is the flute that belonged to Krishna. It has been passed on through generations of my family to keep it safe so that it may one day be given to the chosen one. You, Princess Asha, are the chosen one. This flute now belongs to you," Aadesh explained.

"I don't understand, why would anyone keep a flute for so long?" Asha asked with much confusion in her voice. "How do you know all of this? Krishna has been dead for thousands of years. He is meant to be a myth. That is what has been taught and known to man for thousands of years."

She sat back down, not knowing how to take in all of this information. She could no longer figure out what was truth and what was myth. Why would a poor farmer have the knowledge and a very special antique which once belonged to Krishna?

"My ancestors have been the protectors of Krishna's flute since he died. They brought the people here to the Himalayas. When the oldest child is born from each generation, at the age of sixteen they are sworn to secrecy and sworn to oath that they will protect this flute with their life.

It was written in prophecy that a princess, a descendant of Krishna, would be born and that she would be the chosen one," Aadesh said.

"On the day of your birth, I received a sign Princess. Please take this flute and hide it where no one can find it. You will know when it's time for your journey to begin. Until then the flute must stay hidden."

"Why is this flute so important?" Asha asked. "Why must I have it?"

"You must go, before your attendants realize you are gone." Aadesh escorted Asha to the gates and sent her on her way back to the palace.

The princess made it safely into her room without anyone noticing she was gone. She went into her closet and looked for a hiding place for the flute. There were some boxes in the back of her closet with old stuffed toys inside them. Asha emptied the biggest container and put the box containing the flute at the bottom. Just as she was about to put the stuffed toys on top to hide the box, the princess wondered, *if I slide my fingers across the snake would it open for me?* So she gave it a try, and as she glided her fingers across the snake, the box lit up and then opened. Asha dropped the box and jumped back.

The snake didn't light up for Aadesh, so why did it light up for me? She thought. Asha closed the flute box and put it away at the bottom of her junk box. As she was putting her old toys on top of it, Nisha walked into the room.

"Your Highness, are you in here?" she called.

"I'm in here," Asha yelled. "Just looking for dinner attire." She slid the box into the back of her closet so that no one would suspect anything was out of the ordinary. As she walked out of her closet, her nanny was standing there waiting for her with some new books in her hands.

"Here you go, these arrived for you today. You have a busy week of reading ahead of you. You had best get started on them tomorrow morning."

"Ugh, why me?" Asha said as she fell backwards onto her bed. Nisha left the room and Asha got ready to join her parents for their regular Sunday night dinner together as a family.

Chapter 3 - The Name

Princess Asha awoke early the next morning. She wanted to work on her studies, so that she could go back to the farm to see her new pet cow. With everything else going on, Asha had completely forgotten to give her pet a name. She took out some ink and a feathered pen and started writing down names, starting with A, and went through the alphabet.

Asha couldn't concentrate on anything, not her studies, not a name and not even Dwarka. She lay down on her bed, rubbing her eyes with exhaustion, trying to keep her mind blank. She just couldn't clear her head of the revelations that Aadesh had told her.

Is this all a dream? Will I wake up tomorrow morning and none of this will have happened? Asha thought. She couldn't concentrate, so decided to head to the farm instead of continuing with her studies. As she was sneaking out of the palace and walking through the markets, Asha saw a man trying to sell some jewels.

"Najeena, that will be her name," she shouted out loud. As Asha looked around her, she realized that everyone was looking at her. Embarrassed by this, she ran as quickly as she could through the market and over the hills to the farm.

Princess Asha went straight to the barn, grabbed a handful of grain from the large barrel, and went over to the pastures to give the food to her calf. She sat down next to her and stroked the calf's head.

"You are my precious jewel and that is why I'm naming you Najeena," Asha said as she wrapped her arms around her little furry neck. "I promise that I will always take care of you. I will never neglect you."

Asha stood up and started over the hills, walking towards a beautiful lake. When they got to the edge, Asha sat down and Najeena lay next to her. Asha couldn't stop thinking about Dwarka; she couldn't understand why it needed to be raised again. *If it really exists, should it not be left at the bottom of the ocean?* she thought. "How would I raise a whole island city again anyway? I don't have any magical powers," Asha said out loud.

"That is true, you do not," a voice said from behind. Asha turned around to see who had spoken and saw Aadesh standing behind her.

"I thought I might find you here," he continued as he sat down next to the princess. "So, have you come up with a name for her?" he asked while petting the calf's face. "I see you have become fond of one another."

"Najeena, is what I am naming her," Asha replied. "I hope that you like it."

"It's not for me to like, but yes, I think it's perfect," he said. "Why do you look so gloomy? You have not seemed quite yourself lately, my dear!"

"All of this destiny talk is very overwhelming. I honestly don't know how to take it all in. Why wouldn't anyone tell me about Krishna if I'm his descendant? It's a big important piece of my family history that has been kept secret for thousands of years." the princess replied as she started to throw little rocks into the lake. "It just all seems too unbelievable, Sea Gods and demons, islands sinking under water never to be seen again. It just doesn't sound right," she continued, looking very confused.

"Nothing is always as it seems, Your Highness. You must forever be aware of what and who is around you. Evil has existed since the dawn of time. Gods and demons have always fought throughout the universe. With good there is always bad," Aadesh said. "Everything in life has a purpose, even those rocks that you are throwing into the lake."

"Nisha said that none of this exists, that it is all crazy talk," said Asha, petting Najeena.

"Listen to your heart and make decisions, don't ever be confused by someone else's advice. Your heart's voice is the true voice," advised the farmer.

"We all have that voice inside of us, the one we should always listen to, but most of us are too scared. Ignoring our true inner self is when we find ourselves in trouble. Haven't you ever felt that there is something more out there? Something more that you should be doing? Where we came from and why we are here?"

"Yes, I have felt that ever since I can remember," answered Asha.

"Then you need to embrace that. Whatever you feel inside, the voice that speaks to you from within is what you need to listen to," Aadesh said, holding out his hand to help the princess up. "You need to trust that voice and beware of anyone who tries to stop you, because that is the evil that doesn't want to see you succeed," he added as he turned toward the barn. They both started walking back to the farm to herd the cows into the stalls for milking.

Asha looked back and called for Najeena to come along. Najeena was busy sniffing the fresh grass. When she heard Asha's voice, she looked up and ran over to Asha's side as best she could with her young legs. The sun was setting quickly as they walked up to the main gate of the farm. Asha hugged Aadesh, wrapped her arms around Najeena and gave her a kiss goodbye.

"See you tomorrow!" the princess cried out. Aadesh and Najeena stood at the gate watching the princess walk over the hills until they could no longer see her.

The farmer and Najeena headed back to the barn. As they got closer they could see a figure standing in the doorway. It was the old lady from the village waiting to speak with Aadesh.

"Her journey must begin soon," the old lady said, hobbling alongside whilst the farmer did his chores.

"Time is running out. If she doesn't leave soon, she will never be able to fulfill her destiny."

"The princess cannot undertake this journey until she understands what she is fighting for," Aadesh replied as he was putting hay into the stables. "Asha needs to know who she really is, that she is the pure of heart that the Sea God will listen to," he continued. "If she doubts herself, she will not be able to summon him."

The old lady started to walk slowly out of the barn and turned to Aadesh, holding her head up to him. "You must help her understand soon, or we will all be doomed. The evil is everywhere, and soon we won't be able to stop it." The old lady turned around and hobbled out of the barn, heading back to the village.

The sunrise was bright the next morning; the day was looking to be a beautiful one as Asha got up and opened her tall red velvet curtains. She looked outside to see what was going on.

“You are up early again, Your Highness,” said Nisha as she walked into Asha’s room.

Asha turned around quickly and was startled. She was not expecting her attendant to walk in.

“Yes, Nisha, I’m about to get ready and go to the library,” Asha said with a guilty look on her face. Nisha looked at her in disbelief, knowing that she was up to something.

Asha dressed quickly and headed up to the library. She thought it would be best to go up there for a little while, just in case she was followed. As Asha was going through some of the books, she noticed one was about Krishna defeating the evil demons. Intrigued, she took the book to the corner of the room and started flicking through the pages.

The princess stopped when she saw a picture drawn of an evil-looking woman who was trying to kill Krishna as a baby by trying to poison his breast milk. Asha read how this demon used venom from a snake to poison baby Krishna, but she failed and Krishna defeated her by sucking the life out of the demon woman.

Asha thought that if she could be a descendant to this godlike Krishna, then couldn't there be descendants of these evil demons too? Asha started to feel a bit scared, so she closed the book, put it in her bag, and snuck out of the palace to get to the farm. Asha ran into the barn to look for Aadesh and Najeena, but couldn't find either of them. She ran into the pastures to look for them there. They were nowhere to be found, so she ran over the hills.

In the distance, she could see them both sitting by the lake. As Asha got closer, she noticed that Aadesh was not moving. She walked in front of him and touched him on his shoulder. He opened his eyes and said, "Ah, Asha, Namaste."

"What were you doing?" Asha questioned.

"I was meditating," he replied. "It is something that you should learn to do."

"What is meditating?" Asha asked. "How do you do it?"

"Meditation is relaxing your mind and taking yourself within, learning who you are on the inside and getting away from the material things that exist on the outside," Aadesh explained simply.

"It takes practice and you need to be in a quiet place to get to where you want to be mentally," he continued, staring at the princess and knowing something was bothering her.

"Princess Asha, why do you look so concerned?" he asked.

"I found this book in the library. It was about Krishna and demons this time, not the romantic stories that I've read before," Asha said, looking wide-eyed.

"Okay, and this has concerned you because...?"

"If I'm the descendant of this godlike Krishna—" the princess went on until the farmer stopped her.

"Krishna is a god, not godlike," he corrected her. "Please continue."

"What if there are descendants of these demons living on earth now? What if they are evil, with powers?" the princess said, sounding very frightened. "I can't fight them, I don't have powers."

"Asha, you must remember that Krishna lives inside of you. You can be confident that he will protect you always. You just need to listen to the voice inside; that voice is Krishna," Aadesh said as he stood up and put his hands onto her shoulders.

"You must start your journey to the ocean very soon. You must be at the ocean side of Gujarat before the next blue supermoon in two months."

"What do I do when I get there?" Asha asked.

"You will know what to do. You must remember to listen to the voice inside of you," he said. "There will be many tests along the way. These tests, if you pass them, will make you stronger and wiser."

"Okay, I think I'm ready to take on this task. You can start teaching me all that I need to know starting first thing tomorrow morning," Asha said, standing up taller with more confidence.

Asha and Aadesh got together every day of the following weeks to prepare for her journey to the Sea God. He taught her how to meditate so that she could connect with the universe and her inner-self. Soon enough it was time for Asha to start her journey to Gujarat.

Aadesh said his goodbyes and wished her luck.

"Take Najeena with you," he said, "She is still very young so be patient with her. She will bring you comfort on your travels." He gave Princess Asha and Najeena a hug before they left to head back to the palace, where Asha hid Najeena in the stables.

That night, Asha prepared for her journey. She packed a backpack with some food, a container of water, the book on Krishna and the flute. Once she had packed her bag, she got into bed and tried really hard to fall asleep. There was so much weighing on her mind. There was fear, excitement and anxiety all going through her at once. How could anyone sleep in such a situation? After tossing and turning for a while, the princess finally closed her tired eyes and fell asleep.

Chapter 4 - The Journey

The sun was about to rise and the roosters started to crow. Princess Asha realized that it was time to get up and to sneak out of the palace with Najeena to start her quest to raise Dwarka. Asha picked-up her backpack that she had hidden under her bed and headed down to the palace stables. The princess tiptoed past the stable hands, asleep in their quarters. Asha grabbed Najeena and left through the back entrance, so that nobody could hear her little hooves knocking across the pavement.

As they left the palace gates, Asha jumped as she felt a wrinkly old hand grab her around her wrist and pull her into a dark alley. Asha stood startled, staring at someone in a brown hooded cloak. The person pulled the hood off of her head and handed Asha a peacock feather. It was the old lady from the village.

"Take this feather and keep it close to your heart. It will help you when you need it most," the old lady said to Asha as she put the feather into her hand.

"Um, okay," Princess Asha said, feeling very weird about the feather and the old lady.

"You will be put through many tests along your journey. What you think might be, isn't always what you think it is at all." The old lady was pointing her wrinkly old finger up at Asha's face and continued. "Trust your heart, it is the only thing that speaks the truth."

Asha felt very confused as she turned and walked away from the old lady. As she left the dark alley, she looked back over her shoulder. The old lady was gone; just the cloak was left on the ground where she had stood. *Where did she go? She moves fast for an old lady,* Asha thought. *And why does she always speak in riddles?*

Asha and Najeena headed for the hills toward Mount Kailash. It was starting to get hot as the sun rose and the middle of the day was soon upon them. She decided to stop at the fresh water lake to drink. Princess Asha looked up to see if she could see the Mountain.

"It looks farther away than before. Just when I thought we were getting closer," she said to Najeena.

After a half hour of rest and a drink of water, Asha and Najeena got back up and headed on their way. As they were passing a forest, there was a rustling in the trees. They both looked over to see what was making the noise. Asha's heart was racing as the sounds got louder and closer. All of a sudden something big flew out of the trees and over their heads.

"An owl, during the day?" Asha questioned. "That's weird," she said, looking at Najeena.

As they continued on their journey toward Mount Kailash, they noticed that this beautiful white female owl was following them. Asha started wondering whether she should be worried. As she looked up at the owl sitting on a tree above her, she realized that there was something familiar about this owl; she was giving Asha a very peaceful feeling. Asha started to feel protected and safe with the owl by her side, even if it was just a coincidence that the owl was there.

After a day and a half of walking, the three of them finally reached a village at the bottom of Mount Kailash. They were welcomed with warm drinks and food. The villagers took Najeena to the lake where they bathed and fed her. The people were too poor to have a barn, so they took a bale of hay and made a bed for Najeena with a blanket to help keep her warm. They gave Princess Asha her own cottage to sleep in to make it more comfortable for her. Asha asked one of the wives who was helping her get into bed, "Why are you doing all of this for us? How did you know that we were coming?"

"We know who you are, Your Highness. We have been waiting a long time for you to come. The chosen one has been talked about for many centuries in our village," the beautiful lady said. "You will be the one to save us all. You will end Kali Yuga."

"Kali Yuga, what does that mean?" the princess questioned.

"We are living in the Dark Ages, Your Highness, where evil is all around us and growing fast. We know that you will be the one to get rid of the evil and lead us out of this Dark Age," she said as she wrapped Asha up in the blanket.

"Goodnight Princess, we will have breakfast ready for you in the morning." She closed the door and left Princess Asha to rest.

Asha woke up the next morning with a long, sticky tongue licking her face. She opened her eyes and saw big brown eyes staring back at her.

"Najeena, thanks for the bath," Asha said whilst getting herself out of bed. "We need to start getting ready to leave and head up the mountain," she said as she was packing her bag.

As they left the cottage, they looked around and saw the villagers waiting to give the princess a little something each. Some handed her food, some gave her water. A little girl handed her a blanket that she had made. The final gift was from the beautiful lady from last night who gave Princess Asha a gold bracelet with an amulet on it.

"Keep this around your wrist, Your Highness. It will bring you strength and safety when you need it," the lady said as she closed the clasp of the bracelet around Asha's wrist.

"Your Highness, we are all indebted to you." The lady grabbed Asha by the hand and added quietly, "You are not alone on this journey and you will always have help when you ask for it." They hugged each other goodbye. The princess, Najeena and the owl headed up Mount Kailash.

It took them all day just to travel a quarter of the way up the mountain. It had been a long and tiring journey in the heat, so Asha decided to rest for the night. She took the blanket that the little girl had given her out of her bag, spread it across the dirt, and lay down on it. Najeena lay down next to her so that they could keep each other warm in the damp darkness. The owl perched on a rock and kept a look-out while they slept.

After a few hours of sleep, Asha was woken by a loud screeching. She sat up to see what was going on. The owl was flying around in a panic, making loud hooting noises. Asha saw a shadow across the rock on the mountain and quickly turned to see what it was. It looked like somebody wearing a long, brown hooded cloak, moving like the wind up the mountain. Asha and Najeena stood up quickly, grabbed their belongings, and tried to chase after this person. They ran as fast as they could, but it was too late; whoever it was moved too quickly. Asha sat down, trying to catch her breath, and drank some water from her container. She then poured some water into the top of her container to give to Najeena.

"Who or what was that?" Asha asked.

The owl looked at her with its big yellow eyes as if wanting to say something, but couldn't. "Why would anyone run so quickly up this mountain in the middle of the night?" Asha continued and decided to set-up camp for the second time that night.

Asha was woken at sunrise by the bright, fiery sun shining in her eyes. She sat up and rubbed the sleepiness out of her eyes, took her water bottle, and splashed a little water on her face to help wake up. She packed up her belongings and they started to climb again.

There was something strange about this mountain, but she couldn't put her finger on it. Asha remembered that she had brought one of her books with her that she had not yet finished reading. The princess decided to take a break, took her book out and turned to the pages that spoke of Mount Kailash.

Apparently, nobody had ever completed the journey up to the top! It was written that this mountain belonged to a god named Shiva. When you reach the highest part of the mountain, you would be put through a test. Only people of a strong mind and pure heart would pass this test, Asha read.

"That's it?" she said out loud.

"Seriously! I have to wait to see what the test is going to be? Not one person who made it to the top could have written down what the test is? Ugh!" Asha slammed the book closed, picked-up her bags and started hiking up the mountain once again.

Another long day passed and the clouds were starting to thicken. There was snow that was getting deeper and harder to walk through. Asha decided to call it a day and set up camp again for the night. The night was becoming so cold that Najeena and Asha had to cuddle up to one another again to keep warm. It took two hours for Asha to finally warm up and fall asleep.

The next morning, the bright sun was shining again in Asha's face. As she opened her eyes, she could see two shadows in front of her. She rubbed her tired eyes to wake herself up and the shadows became clearer. There were two men that she recognized from the village at the bottom of the mountain, both anxiously trying to speak.

"Your Highness, Your Highness," the men said together.

"It's your royal nanny. She was in the village looking for you, then she disappeared and nobody can find her."

"Did anyone tell her where I was headed?" Asha asked.

"No, Your Highness, we did try to stall her with food and water, but then she was gone," one of the men said.

Asha stood up, collected her things, and spoke again.

"It's okay, let's not panic. Maybe she went back to the palace. You should head home back to your families and I will continue up the mountain."

The men gave what was left of their water to Asha and headed back down the mountain to their village. The princess, Najeena, and the owl continued their cold and tiresome journey up Mount Kailash.

Half a day had already passed and the three were nearly at the top of the mountain. As they moved closer to the top, Asha's ears were starting to hurt. She drank some water, hoping it would take away the pain, but it continued to worsen the closer that they got to the top.

The ringing in her ears was becoming unbearable and Asha cried in pain.

“I can’t do this, it hurts too much,” she cried out. Tears were rolling down her face as she covered her ears, trying to control the ringing, but there was nothing that she could do.

Najeena nudged Asha from behind, forcing her to keep moving forward.

Finally, they reached the top of the mountain and suddenly the pain in her ears went away. Now it was time for them to walk around and down the other side.

“Was that the test?” Asha asked out loud.

“Did I actually pass the test?” she asked, looking at the owl and Najeena. The owl shook its head and the princess lost all of her excitement. Asha was frowning, scared of what she would find on the other side of the mountain.

As they continued, fog started to appear, which made it difficult for them to see anything in front of them. From nowhere, Asha could hear a voice.

"Asha, my sweet child, please do not go." It was the voice of her mother. Just as Asha was about to turn around to see if her mother was behind her, she heard another voice.

"You will be put through many tests. Whatever you do, stay strong and keep going." This time it was the voice of the old lady from her village. Asha decided not to turn around and pressed on.

"Asha, you must come home. I'm very sick. I need you by my side." It was the voice of her father but weak and sickly sounding.

"Father," Asha cried out. "My father is sick, I must go back." The owl flapped frantically in front of Asha to prevent her from turning around.

"Stop! I have to go back," Asha shouted at the owl. Najeena kept nudging her forward, Asha was getting angry with them both.

"Your Highness, remember who you are, remember your destiny." This time it was the voice of Aadesh whom Asha trusted with all her heart. Asha took a few deep breaths and realized that this was the test. *I have to overcome the cries of the people who mean the most to me.* As soon as Asha realized that this was the test, the fog started to clear and they were finally on the other side of the mountain.

As the last clouds of fog lifted away, they could see a figure standing in front of them. Asha squinted to see if she could recognise who it was. As they walked closer, she realised that it was her nanny.

“Nisha,” Asha stuttered. “What are you doing here? How did you get up here so fast?”

“I’ve come to take you home, Your Highness,” Nisha replied. “Why are you climbing this mountain? What are you looking for?”

“It was you that ran past me when I was sleeping, wasn’t it?” asked Asha. Before Nisha could answer her question, the princess continued, “I’m sorry, but I have to continue this journey, it is my destiny," the princess said sternly.

"Why are you talking such madness? Your destiny is to become queen and that is it," Nisha said with a wicked chuckle.

"Let's go, I'm taking you home. Your parents are worried sick."

"If my parents are so worried about me, then where are the guards? Why are you here alone?" Asha asked.

"Princess Asha, enough with the questions and let's go," Nisha said, trying to grab hold of the princess's arm.

In an instant, the owl swooped in between Asha and Nisha. They both fell to the ground, and the owl hooked her claws into Nisha and held her down.

"Get off of me, you wretched animal," she screamed, swinging her arms around, trying to dislodge the owl. "Asha, help get this thing off me."

"No, and it's not a thing. She is an owl and she is my friend," said Asha. "I'm sorry, but I'm not going back with you."

The fog started to re-appear and Asha could hear a hissing that sounded like a snake. A dark cloud started to form above Asha's head, the hissing was now above her.

"Your Highness, behind you!" shouted Nisha.

Asha was too scared to look up. The owl flew away from Nisha and over to the princess. “Come over to me Asha, I will protect you,” Nisha said.

Asha turned around and looked up. There hovering over her was a ten-headed serpent. She screamed, walking backward, tripping over the rocks.

“We have been waiting for you, Princess,” the serpents said. “You must destroy Nisha. She is evil.”

“What? I can’t harm her. She is my royal attendant and has looked after me all of my life,” said Asha.

The serpents slithered closer to Asha, “You must, before she destroys you.”

"Don't listen to them Asha, they are lying," Nisha cried out. "Look at them, they are talking serpents; you cannot trust them."

"Ask her to come closer, Princess," the serpents told Asha.

"This is sacred ground and a demon cannot come closer. She cannot come through here. Mount Kailash belongs to the gods, and only those who are pure of heart may pass," the ten-headed snake said, slithering around the mountain floor.

Asha was feeling very overwhelmed. She couldn't fathom a talking snake, let alone a ten-headed talking one. Who was she to trust? What was the real reason for Nisha being on top of the mountain? How did she get here so quickly? There were so many questions running through Asha's head.

"I need to continue, you must let me through Nisha. I demand that you let me through," Asha said in her strongest regal voice.

"I'm sorry, Your Highness, but I can't let you continue," Nisha said, looking into Asha's eyes.

"You can't stop me," Asha said.

"I can and I will," Nisha said as she started to grow into a giant creature with fangs and yellow eyes. Her fingernails turned into claws, her tongue became long and pointy.

The owl grabbed onto the back of Asha and pulled her away from this giant monster. The serpent slid in front of Asha, the owl and Najeena to protect them.

"Take a tooth and stab her with our venom. This will poison her so that you can escape," the ten-headed serpent said.

The monster tried to grab Asha with her giant arms, but couldn't reach without falling onto the sacred ground. Instead, she grabbed hold of Najeena and threw her against the rocks on the mountain.

"Najeena!" Asha cried out, but fortunately the calf did not appear hurt, just winded. The owl tried to stall Nisha by flapping her wings into the demon's face. As Najeena struggled to her feet and ambled towards her, Asha grabbed a tooth from one of the snakes' mouths and ran as fast as she could toward this demonic giant.

She slid across the ground and stabbed her in the foot with the serpent's tooth. The demon screamed out in pain, tripped over a rock and rolled to the bottom for miles and miles like a giant ball. She lay motionless until the villagers, who looked like tiny ants, came and stood over her lifeless body.

Asha looked up at the serpents in shock.

"Can you please explain to me what just happened?" she asked, hugging Najeena. "Nisha has been my most trusted servant since the day I was born. How could I not have known that she was evil?"

"Evil is all around us, Princess, we cannot escape from it. You cannot always see it because it isn't always what or whom you think it is. Evil is very deceiving," the serpents said to Asha as they slithered around her.

Asha was feeling a little uncomfortable with them getting too close. *Who could she trust now that she had been betrayed by Nisha?* Asha felt an overwhelming sadness in her heart that she could not save her nanny from the darkness.

“You must complete your destiny so that good can prevail,” they said as they got close to her face, looking into her big brown eyes.

“Where am I supposed to go from here?” Asha asked the serpents with hesitation in her voice. “We are so far away from where Dwarka is meant to be,” she said.

“You must go to the sacred Lake Manasarovar and collect water from the lake. Make sure that you keep this water safe,” the serpents told her.

“You will then head to the river Yamuna. You will need to make yourself a raft to travel down the river and all of the rivers that connect to each other heading to the west coast. You must reach Gujarat before the blue supermoon ends," the serpents said slithering around her.

"Once you reach the coast of Gujarat you must drink the water and summon the Sea God."

As the serpents slithered away into the fog, Asha cried out to them, "How do I summon the Sea God?"

"You will know what to do when the time comes," they replied in the distance.

Asha took a long deep breath, gathered all of her belongings, and headed back down the mountain. The princess gazed over the rocky edge to watch the woman she had once trusted being carried away by the villagers.

It was twice as fast getting down the mountain as it was going up. It was a good thing that Asha and Najeena had found their new owl friend to help guide them. Princess Asha had never traveled outside of her kingdom; she had no idea where she was going.

The days rolled by and the party of three finally reached Lake Manasarovar. The owl flew around the lake fast and fiercely. She dove into the water and back out as if she were the happiest bird in the world. Asha watched in amazement, wishing that she had the power and confidence of this magnificent bird that had chosen to stay by her side throughout this quest.

Asha splashed some water onto her face and washed her arms and hands. She took her ponytail out, washed her lovely long dark brown hair in the water and flipped it back into a bun. She took a large water bottle out of her backpack and started to fill it with water, just as the serpent had told her to. As Asha was filling up her bottle, a face appeared in the water in front of her. This face made Asha jump back from the lake and look over her shoulder to see if anyone was standing there, but there was nobody. She looked back again and saw the face smiling at her. It was the face of Krishna. Asha stared at him for a while, feeling at peace and confident, until the image faded away as quickly as it had appeared.

It was time to move on and she decided to put the water bottle around her neck using the strap to keep it safe and close. Najeena took a long drink from the lake before running in and having a good splash around to cool herself off. It was a welcome break from all of the hours of walking.

"It's time to go," Asha shouted. "We have to get to the river before dark."

The owl flew ahead of Asha and Najeena so that they could follow in the right direction. When they reached the river, Asha and Najeena looked for as many pieces of wood as they could find so that they could build a raft. *What will I use to keep the wood together?* Asha thought. As she was looking around to figure out what she could use as rope, the owl came swooping down with long, strong vines from the trees surrounding the edge of the river.

"Perfect! You are amazing, thank you," Asha said as she scratched the owl's head in appreciation. "Let's build us a raft!" She excitedly went through all the pieces of wood that they had gathered.

The princess spent hours building a raft strong enough to hold herself and Najeena, with the owl flying back and forth with large vines to tie the wood planks together. Just when Asha thought she was finished, the owl came flying down with a huge palm leaf.

"What am I supposed to do with that?" Asha asked. The owl flew above the raft, holding the large palm leaf as shade.

"You are so clever, of course we need cover from the sun and the rain," Asha said, smiling at the owl.

Asha tied four pieces of wood on the raft to make posts and then some across to make a support to put the large palm leaf on.

"I think we might need one larger palm leaf," she said to the owl. She flew back into the forest and returned with another large leaf.

"Wow, you can understand everything I say. I will never cease to be amazed." Asha said to the owl in astonishment.

"I think that we are ready to travel down the river."

Najeena and Asha pushed the raft into the water. The river was moving quite rapidly, so the owl held onto the raft so that Asha could put her belongings and Najeena onto it.

That done, when they were all aboard, Asha pushed the raft off from the shore and jumped onto it herself. They were finally on their way to Gujarat to raise Dwarka. None of them knew what to expect in the next few days of this journey. Asha took several deep breaths, picked-up the oar that she had made from a tree branch, and they headed down the river into the sunset.

Chapter 5 - The Beast

Hours soon passed and Asha and Najeena fell asleep as the raft was floating downriver. They were woken up by splashes of water on their faces. The raft had drifted to the edge and had become stuck in some large rocks. The water rushing down was splashing over the raft, making Asha and Najeena very wet. Asha jumped onto her feet in a panic.

"Where are we?" she cried out. The owl flew above and was facing an adjoining river, the one that Asha was meant to go down in order to get to the west coast. Asha took her oar and pushed them off the rocks. They headed back across the river and made the turn onto the adjoining flow.

The owl flew ahead to direct the way when, all of a sudden, she swooped into the river and grabbed a huge fish. She came onto the raft and started to eat. Asha and Najeena looked at each other in disgust. Watching the owl tear apart the fish with its beak was not pleasant viewing.

The raft started to slow down a little as the water became calmer and the river got a little wider. They were all sitting quietly enjoying the ride until there was a nudge on the raft. Asha stood up.

"What was that?" There was a nudge again, but this time so hard that it nearly knocked Asha overboard. She was frantically looking all about to see what was banging into their raft, but couldn't see anything.

As the princess kneeled over the back of the raft, a huge mouth full of teeth opened up and tried to grab her. It wasn't successful, but it grabbed a hold of the string of the bottle and pulled Asha into the water. She quickly broke the string, grabbed hold of the bottle and swam toward the raft as quickly as she could.

"It's a huge crocodile," she screamed. The owl started to flap her wings in front of the crocodile to distract it.

All of a sudden Asha was pulled under the water; the crocodile had her by the ankle. Fighting under the water, Asha hit it over the head with her water bottle, but nothing was working. Najeena jumped into the water to get the crocodile's attention.

It let go of Asha's leg and started to swim after Najeena. Asha swam up to the top of the water and gasped for air. When she finally caught her breath, she screamed, "Najeena, get out of the water."

The owl flew after the raft so that it didn't float away. Najeena got up onto the grass and Asha grabbed hold of a rock sticking out of the water. She was trying to catch her breath and climb, but she was wounded by a bite from the crocodile.

The crocodile was still chasing after Najeena.

"Run Najeena, run," Asha screamed. She finally got to the side and was able to pull herself up onto the grass. Najeena ran over and nudged her head under Asha's arm to help her up. They both ran as fast as they could to get away from the crocodile.

“Run in a zigzag, Najeena, it confuses them,” Asha called.

A loud roar came from the trees and a lion came running out. It stopped, looked at Asha and Najeena and then dashed for the crocodile. This large, beautiful beast grabbed the crocodile by its tail and swung it up against a tree. The lion then looked back at Asha and Najeena, who were staring in shock. The lion looked at them as if to say, *Run, I’ve got this*. The two of them ran as fast as they could. They caught up to the raft and the owl, jumped back on, and headed down the river.

“Don’t mess with the king of the jungle!” Asha said to Najeena.

Asha was still bleeding from her wounded ankle and needed something to tie around it. She looked through her bag and found a cloth that was keeping some of her food wrapped up. She put the food to the side and wrapped the cloth around her ankle. When she looked up, the owl was standing in front of her with the bottle of water from the sacred lake.

"What do you want me to do with that?" Asha asked. The owl pointed the bottle to her ankle.

"I can't use this water on my wound. I need it to summon the Sea God," Asha said. The owl insisted she pour some of the water on her wound.

"Okay I will put just a little on it." The princess took the bottle from the owl, removed the cloth, and poured a bit onto her ankle.

"Arrrhhhh, that hurts," Asha cried out. The owl looked at her and then looked down at the wound. "It's healing it," Asha said in amazement. "The water is healing my wound, this is amazing!" She put the top back on the bottle and placed it in her bag to keep the rest of the sacred water safe.

It had been a long day for the three of them, it was getting dark and they were tired and hungry. Asha decided to stop the raft and pull it up onto the edge of the river and look for somewhere to rest and find food. As they walked across the fields of grass and through a forest they saw a village in the distance.

"I think we should head to the village and hope that they welcome us with open arms," Asha said.

As they got closer, the people stood and stared as the three of them entered into their village. "Is anyone going to say anything to us?" Asha whispered to Najeena.

"Welcome, Princess Asha," a strong male voice said, coming from one of the larger homes. "Please come in out of the dampness and make yourselves at home," the man said.

"Thank you," Asha responded hesitantly. "How do you know my name?"

"Please, Your Highness, we all know who you are. Word travels fast around here. You are the one who is going to save us all from the Kali Yuga and bring us into a new world of love and peace. I am the chief of this village. I make sure my people are safe and always have food and water," the chief explained to Asha.

"Wow, I didn't realize I was that famous," Asha said cheekily.

"Let us get you some food and a place to sleep for the night," said the chief.

"That is very kind of you, but just some food and water would be wonderful. We won't need a bed for the night. We are going to be on our way in several hours," Asha said to the chief.

"Nonsense, Your Highness. You need to rest to build up your energy for the rest of your journey. I insist. I have a comfortable room for you to stay in, fit for a queen," the chief insisted.

Princess Asha finished the meal that was prepared for her by the villagers and got up to check on Najeena, who was in one of the stalls eating hay. Asha couldn't stop yawning, so she decided it would be a good idea to get a good night's sleep and to take the room that the chief had offered to her.

Chapter 6 - The Traitor

Asha was woken in the morning by a very loud noise. It was Najeena fighting off the villagers who were trying to put a halter on her and take her away. Asha looked out the window and saw Najeena kicking and screeching to get the people off of her. Asha tried to open the window to shout out to the villagers to stop, but she couldn't get it open. She quickly put on the rest of her clothes and ran to the door. It was locked from the outside!

Banging and kicking the door, Asha screamed for help.

“Please open the door, help me.” Nobody was listening, so Asha tried to kick the door down again, but nothing was working. She started to cry, leaning up against the door.

“Somebody please help me.” All of a sudden there was a bang against the window. It was the owl trying to get in. “Go and get help,” Asha begged. The owl nodded to Asha as if it understood what she was saying and flew off.

Asha waited helplessly, wondering if she had imagined the owl nodding to her. All she could think of was Najeena and how she had failed to protect her. Asha sat on the floor, put her head between her knees, and sobbed in desperation.

Minutes later, Asha heard a voice in the other room that sounded like the chief. “Let me out of here,” she shouted.

“I’m sorry, Your Highness, but I cannot,” the chief said.

“Why not?” Asha said very sternly.

“I cannot let you reach the Sea God. I cannot let you fulfill your destiny,” he answered.

“You are one of the demons, the evil of the world, aren’t you?” Asha asked.

“You are very clever for a young princess. I am a loyal servant of the darkness, and I will not allow you to leave. The blue supermoon will come and it will be too late for you,” he said with an evil laugh.

“You will not get away with this. Good always overcomes evil,” Asha replied.

The chief laughed again. "It doesn't seem to be winning right now, Princess." He walked away, still chuckling. Asha curled up on the floor and cried.

About an hour later, the owl flew past the window. Following it was a bull charging across to help. *A bull?* Asha thought. *What is a bull going to do?*

BANG! The door came crashing down and the bull ran inside. He swept up Princess Asha onto his back and took off through the village, knocking down anything and anyone who got in his way.

"Wait, stop!" screamed Asha. "We need to get Najeena, she is in trouble." The bull halted, but the owl insisted they continue.

"I can't leave her," Asha said. The chief started to charge after them with a huge pitchfork and some of his village people following behind with their own large farming tools, ready to attack Asha and her animal tribe.

"You will not get away, Princess," he shouted to her. "I will not let you finish your quest."

"Run!" Asha shouted to the bull. He ran as fast as he could over the fields and across the farms, following the owl to safety. They finally got into the forest, far away from the evil villagers. Asha jumped off the bull and petted his head as a thank-you for saving her. She looked back toward the village with a tear rolling down her cheek.

"I have to go back and save Najeena. I cannot leave her," Asha said softly, her heart filled with sadness, wondering what had become of her only friend. The owl nudged Asha to turn around and walk farther into the forest.

“No, I will not leave her behind,” Asha yelled. The owl nudged her some more. Asha wouldn’t budge, so the owl grabbed her arm with its huge claws and pulled the princess into the forest.

“Stop pulling me, I’m going back for Najeena. You can come and help or you can stay,” she said, trying to resist the powerful owl.

As they moved deeper into the forest, they heard some voices. Asha could just make out two people and what looked like a young calf.

“Najeena,” she cried out with excitement. “You are safe.” Asha hugged her friend.

“I don’t understand, why are you here with her? Why did you save Najeena?”

“We were never trying to harm her, Your Highness,” said one of the villagers.

"We knew what the chief was up to and we wanted to help in any way that we could. We believe in you, Princess," the other young male villager said.

"Thank you so much for saving her. I will be truly grateful to you both for the rest of my life," Asha said.

"You will always be welcomed in my kingdom as honored guests." They bowed down to the princess, handed her a cloth full of bread and cheese for her journey, and went on their way back to the village. The bull followed behind them.

The three were alone again and Asha wasn't sure where to go. They were so far away from the river that it would take a day to get back there. The owl flew above the forest to find the direction they needed to head off in. She showed the princess how to get out of the forest and they headed westward toward Gujarat. It would be a blue supermoon in two days and time was running out for them.

"We need to figure out where we are," Asha said.

After hours of walking, they finally left the forest and moved onto a muddy path. There were many wide-open fields and farms. It was serene walking along this path and so peaceful that all you could hear were birds chirping and water from a stream running nearby.

"Look, there is some fresh water we can drink," Asha said, pointing to the stream. She ran down, knelt, and drank the fresh, cool water. Najeena took a nice long drink from the stream and they headed back onto the path to continue their journey.

Chapter 7 - The Whirlwind

It was dark, and the three friends decided to rest in one of the fields under a big beautiful tree with the stream alongside. The picturesque view reminded Asha of a picture she saw in one of her books of Krishna. He was sitting on a swing under a similar tree with his loving wife, his flute in his hand and the stream next to them.

Asha took the flute out of her bag and stared at the box as she thought to herself *how will I know how to play this instrument?* As she looked long and hard at the box that held the flute, she decided to give it a try and opened the box by passing her fingers across the snake. The box lit up and the top flipped open. There it was, one of the oldest, most sacred artifacts in history and it was in her possession.

Asha took the flute out and tried to play it, but no sound came out, just air. She tried again, but still no luck in getting any music out of it. Asha threw herself back against the large tree trunk in frustration. Najeena and the owl both sat there staring at the princess. It was almost as though they were looking thoughtful, wishing that there was something they could do to help her.

"It's useless. All I get is air out of it. I've never played a musical instrument in my life. I'll never be able to summon the Sea God," Asha said, putting her head between her knees. "It's getting late. We should get some rest."

Asha and Najeena made themselves comfortable under the tree, and the owl took off to find some food.

It was the middle of the night and the three of them were fast asleep. All of a sudden, a huge gust of wind came over them. Princess Asha jumped up quickly and grabbed onto the tree trunk. Najeena ran behind the tree to protect herself and the owl was blown away in this strong whirlwind.

"Where is this coming from?" Asha shouted out. From nowhere two long arms came out of this strange tornado, snatched the flute and took off over the pastures.

"My flute," wailed Asha. "It took my flute! What was that?" Asha had never seen anything like it before, so she grabbed her book out of her bag to search for any references that resembled a tornado. As she flicked through the pages, the princess came upon a demon that

Krishna had killed by the name of Trinavarta, the whirlwind demon.

"How can this be? He is dead," Asha asked herself. "We need to find my flute," she said to Najeena, hastily packing everything into her bag.

Heading west on the path, Asha didn't know where to start looking. This demon could be anywhere, and how was she supposed to catch it? It was way too fast for her. They walked for hours in the dark. The only lights that they had to follow were the bright stars shining above them.

The sun started to rise and shed light onto their path. In the distance, there was a barn with fenced-in pastures around it. There was a loud, thumping noise moving past them. Asha looked to the right and saw horses galloping.

"That's it, we can ask for a horse," Asha said excitedly.

Asha approached the young farmer who was sorting out the hay for the horses and cows. "Excuse me, sir, we are in need of a horse. Would you be so kind as to lend us one, your fastest and strongest? You will be greatly rewarded by my kingdom."

"Your Highness," the young farmer said as he knelt down in front of the princess, "it would be an honor to give you the best horse that I have. He is a stallion and the fastest of all of them." The farmer took Asha over to the pasture where the horses were wandering, and about twenty horses galloped over to them. In the middle of the herd was a stunning black stallion with a long white mane and long white tail. He had white socks on the bottom of all four legs. Asha gaped in amazement: she had never seen such beauty in an animal before. This horse was magnificent!

"He is beautiful," Asha said as she stroked his face. "Are you sure you would like to give your most beautiful horse to me?"

"Please, Your Highness, it would be an insult if I did not give you the best of what I have," he replied. "Come, let's saddle him up for you."

They walked the horse into the barn, put his saddle on, then his bridle and gave him an apple as a treat. The farmer put a blanket on the front of the saddle for Najeena to lie across. "He is my gift to you, Princess Asha. Please keep this horse as your own. His name is Spirit, and he will keep you safe from any harm. He is as fast as the wind."

"Perfect, that's what I need. Something to outrun the wind," Asha muttered under her breath. "I thank you kindly. I am indebted to you." They took off on Spirit with the owl flying behind to look for the demon wind.

As they galloped over the fields, Asha could see another forest in the valley below. In the center of that forest she could see trees blowing all over the place, but there was no wind blowing elsewhere. Asha stopped Spirit, and they stood on top of the hill. The owl went to fly above the blowing trees to see if it was, in fact, the demon. The owl quickly flew back and nodded. The demon was in the forest with the flute.

Asha galloped over to the forest as quickly as she could, weaving in between the trees, trying not to hit one. Najeena was so scared that she shut her eyes tight so that she couldn't see how fast they were going.

As they got close to the demon, Asha shouted out, "Give me back my flute!"

Strong male laughter came from inside the whirlwind.

"Never! It belongs to me now," the voice said. The demon's head popped up over the top of the wind as he continued to laugh at all of them. Asha could now get a good look at this creature who had long black hair and a long beard; he was a giant with large muscles. He almost looked like an evil genie from her books.

He sped off deeper into the forest and Asha galloped after him. As she caught up to him, she put her arm into the wind to try to grab the flute. The powerful creature grabbed at the princess in return. He pulled her off the horse and into the center of his whirlwind. Asha fought with all her might to get away. The princess was tiny compared to him, so tiny that he had her wrapped in one hand, squeezing her tight. He was waving the flute in the other hand. Asha was punching him as hard as she could, but he was barely feeling her hits; he was just too big and strong for her.

All of a sudden, the demon started screeching very loudly. The owl had flown into the wind and grabbed his back with her huge claws. The owl kept digging her claws into him until he finally fell to the ground in pain. Asha escaped his grip, ran over to the other hand, grabbed the flute and ran as fast as she could to get away.

Unfortunately, he was able to get hold of her again.

"Let me go!" Asha yelled at him. "How are you still alive, Trinavarta?"

"I am not Trinavarta, I am his descendant. I am here to avenge his death and to stop you from getting to the Sea God," he said angrily. As the giant was getting back to his feet with Asha in one hand and trying to grab the flute with the other, she quickly threw the flute over to the owl.

Just before the giant could chase the flute, with a huge creaking and cracking noise, a huge tree fell on top of him and crushed him. Luckily, the tree missed the hand that Asha was in.

She climbed out of his giant hand, looked over to where the tree had fallen, and saw that Spirit had kicked the tree down with his powerful hind legs. Asha ran quickly over to Spirit and Najeena and hugged them both.

"Thank you so much, I thought I was done for," Asha said with much relief. She climbed back onto Spirit to continue their journey to Gujarat. She put the flute safely back into her bag and they galloped off over the fields into the sunset.

Chapter 8 - Gujarat

They had finally made it. The state was bigger than anything Asha had ever seen before. It had many more people and was a lot more modern too. At last they were in Gujarat and the people were most welcoming to them. It was as if they had been expecting this strange group for a very long time. The weary travelers walked proudly through the towns and headed towards the palace. As they got closer, the large beautiful gates with gold trim opened up to let them in. A handsome young man came running down the grand staircase.

"Princess Asha, welcome to my home," the dazzling young prince said with a bright white smile. "Let my stable hand put your horse in the barn for you and please come and get something to eat. You must be starving!"

Asha couldn't speak. She was in shock at seeing the young prince, whom she had danced with all night at her birthday ball. She also remembered that she had stood the handsome young prince up for breakfast the next morning. Asha did not think she would ever see him again. What was she going to say to him without embarrassing herself? What did he think of her?

"Maybe he's forgotten about me standing him up," Asha mumbled to Najeena.

The young, handsome prince turned around and looked at Asha and said, "By the way, you owe me a breakfast." Asha couldn't help but blush as she smiled back at the prince. "Shall we say tomorrow morning in the gardens?" he asked with a cheeky grin.

"Sure thing," Asha said, smiling from ear to ear.

"I am starving now, maybe we can start with dinner tonight first?" Her eyes were bright and wide.

"Of course, dinner first it is," the prince said with his arm out for the princess to take so that he could escort her into the royal palace. "My staff will show you to your quarters and I will meet you in the dining room for dinner, let's say at sunset?"

"Yes, sunset it is," the princess said, very distracted by the beautiful décor of the palace.

The floors were of a gorgeous marble and the grand stairway was made of mahogany with gold around the bannisters. The ceilings were really high, and there was beautiful art on them. The art was hand-painted and was of all the gods and goddesses. This palace was twice the size of Asha's palace; the gardens were beautifully manicured, and the flowers were enchanting.

"Your Highness, please come this way to your room," a female voice said from behind her. A young servant took the princess up the sweeping staircase and down a long corridor and through some huge double doors. The bedroom was so stunning and perfectly to the taste of Princess Asha; it was like the room had been made just for her.

"I hope you will be comfortable, Your Highness. I will be serving you during your stay, so if there is anything that you need, please do not hesitate to ask."

"Thank you, that is very kind of you," Asha replied. "I think I will be very comfortable here."

The servant girl left and Asha toured her quarters, looking at the tall red velvet curtains and the extra-large marble bathroom accented in gold. She opened the tall double doors that went into a dressing room and hanging in front of her was a beautiful red and gold sari. It was the most beautiful sari that she had ever seen. When Asha walked over to take a better look at it, she saw a note on the hanger. It read, *My beautiful Princess Asha, this sari has been custom-made for you and I would be honored if you would wear it tonight at dinner.* It was signed by the prince, which made Asha smile from ear to ear.

Asha took a long hot bath and was putting on her sari when there was a knock at the door. "Come in," Asha shouted. Her young lady servant came in with some more beautiful things for the princess to wear. She was holding a dark red velvet box; inside of it was a gold, diamond and ruby necklace, with earrings to match.

"Your Highness, the prince has asked me to give these jewels to you. May I please assist you with putting them on?" the servant asked. Asha sat down on the large velvet ottoman so that she could put on her jewelry.

"You look very beautiful, Your Highness. The prince will be very smitten when he sees you," the young servant said as she clipped on the necklace.

"Thank you, but I think it is a bit too much to accept. We have only just met and to accept all of these gifts makes me feel a little uncomfortable," Asha said, feeling a little awkward with all the magnificent gifts. “I guess I should head to the dining room.”

The young servant escorted Asha down to the dining room, where she would meet the king and queen and dine with the handsome young prince of Gujarat.

As Asha walked into the most glamorous dining room that she had ever seen, the prince was having a very serious conversation with his parents, the king and queen of Gujarat.

When they realized that the princess had walked in, the three of them went very quiet.

“Princess Asha, please come in,” the queen said as she walked up to greet her. Asha bowed to the king and queen and thanked them for giving her such a warm welcome into their home.

After a long night of great food and stimulating conversation, Princess Asha decided it was time to rest. The prince offered to escort her back to her room. They both wished the king and queen a good night and headed down the large hallways and up the grand stairwell. As they reached her room, the prince took Asha's hands into his and looked deep into her big brown eyes.

"Asha, I know that you have a big quest that you must finish, but when you have saved the world..." he said, grinning, and then paused. "Do you think that you might have a little time to get to know me better?"

Asha started to squirm a little as she was feeling a little out of her comfort zone; she had never kissed a boy before, let alone had a handsome young prince wanting to spend time with her.

"I would love to spend more time with you, but right now I really need to concentrate on what I'm meant to be doing, my purpose in life," she said, looking into his beautiful green eyes. "I hope that you will wait for me, but I understand if you do not want to."

"Asha, I am eighteen years old, I am in no rush and of course I will wait for you," the prince said. "I will see you in the morning for breakfast!" He kissed her on the cheek, opened her door, gave Asha a bow and walked away.

Asha put a hand on her cheek where the prince had kissed her; she felt weak in her knees. She adored the prince, but she knew that this mission was her priority and that she needed to focus with no distractions.

It is a beautiful morning for breakfast in the garden and a good way to say my goodbyes to the royal family of Gujarat, Asha thought, as she looked outside her extra-large windows. She packed up her things and headed downstairs to breakfast.

As Asha was walking out of her bedroom doors, she bumped into the prince. He was holding a gold necklace that had a beautiful pendant of a lotus flower.

"Your Highness, I'm so sorry, I did not see you there," Asha said, blushing.

"I should not have sneaked up on you Princess. I'm the one who is sorry," the prince said as he bowed down to her. "I wanted to give you a gift, one that I would like you to wear for the final part of your journey."

"You have showered me with enough gifts, Your Highness," Asha said, feeling modest and still a little uncomfortable.

"You must understand Asha, this gift isn't about my feelings for you, it's a gift from the gods. It's very sacred and it will help protect you from any evil that tries to stop you," the prince said in a very serious voice, "It is said that, in your darkest hour, let the lotus be your light. This is a lotus flower and behind the pendant there is a hook. The hook is for a peacock feather, but the peacock feather must also be sacred."

Asha thought for a few moments about where she could find a sacred peacock feather until it occurred to her.

"I have one," she said excitedly. She searched through her bag for the peacock feather that she had been carrying from the old lady from her village. "This was given to me by an old wise woman from my village. She told me it will protect me," Asha said as she put it in the tiny hole on the back of the pendant.

"May I put it around your neck?" the prince asked. Asha gently nodded and turned around to let the prince put the sacred necklace on her.

"It looks beautiful on you Princess. Please take care of it and never let anyone else get hold of it," he said sternly. Asha smiled at him and nodded. "May I escort you to breakfast, my lady?" Asha took his arm, and they walked downstairs for their final meal together.

Najeena and the owl were both waiting by the royal gates, ready to depart and finish their quest. Asha said her goodbyes to the king and queen. The prince kissed her on both of her cheeks and then on her forehead. The stable hand brought Spirit over and helped Asha and Najeena onto his back. They trotted out of the gates, waving goodbye to the royal family as they watched them leave.

Chapter 9 - The Evil Serpent

It was a hot day, and even though the sun was shining bright, you could see the blue supermoon shining brightly too.

"It's the last day of the supermoon, we must get to the Sea God today like the prophecy said!" Asha exclaimed. "We cannot let anything or anyone get in our way." She gently kicked the sides of Spirit to make him gallop as they headed over the hills toward the shoreline.

They were going so fast that the breeze took the peacock feather right out of the pendant. Asha pulled Spirit to a halt and turned him around to chase after the feather that was blowing around in the wind. She was struggling to catch it.

“We don’t have time for this,” she cried. The owl swooped down, finally grabbed a hold of the feather in her claws and flew over to Asha. The princess put it back into the pendant and made sure it was in tighter this time.

“That was a close one, thank you,” Asha said.

They continued on over the hills, but a little slower so that they didn’t lose the feather a second time.

They cantered along a path which ended at the entrance to a cave.

"How are we meant to get through this to continue our journey?" Asha asked. "Nobody ever mentioned a cave to us."

As they got closer to the mountain cave, they could see that there was no way around it. Travelling through was the only option. Asha dismounted Spirit and pulled Najeena off too. She led Spirit by his reins and started to walk through this mysterious cave. They walked very carefully, trying not to slip on the slime on the ground.

"This is so gross," Asha said as she shook off the disgusting slime that dripped onto her arm. "It's darker the farther we go in, and I don't have a lamp," she said, worried.

As they proceeded deeper, the cave started to move and close in on them.

"What is happening?" Asha screamed out.

They ran further into the cave, but there seemed to be no light at the end. The cave moved even more, and the group started to lose their balance and fall all over the place.

"We have to go back, something isn't right," said Asha. They turned around to head back out of the cave, but the entrance had closed itself. The cave started to move across the hills with them inside.

"How are we moving?" Asha screamed again. She suddenly realized that it wasn't a mountain cave they'd walked into, it was alive.

"We need to get out of here! Kick the side as hard as you can," she said to Najeena and Spirit.

"I'll punch and you claw into it," Asha said to the owl. They all worked hard trying to get out of this creature. Nothing was working and they were all getting tired.

"It's useless," Asha said as she sat down in the goo and put her head between her knees.

"I'm never going to see my parents again," she sobbed, "I'm going to fail everybody,"

Najeena went over to her and nudged her head under her arm to comfort her. All of a sudden there was a light from Asha's neck. Najeena stepped back from the princess, a little scared and surprised by this bright light. Asha looked down at the light.

"It's the lotus pendant," she said. *In your darkest hour, let the lotus be your light,* she thought, hearing the prince's voice in her head.

The owl started to frantically flap her wings up against the body of the creature that they were in. Asha looked at the owl, feeling confused at what she was trying to tell her. The owl flew to Asha, grabbed the necklace in her beak, and pulled Asha up toward the body of the creature. Asha took off the necklace and pressed the pendant onto the creature's insides. It started burning a hole in the body! There was hope after all!

The creature screeched in pain as the pendant burned a bigger hole.

"The hole is getting bigger," yelled Asha. "Come on, help open it so that we can get out." They all kicked, punched and clawed their way out of the creature. It was very challenging because it was slithering around so frantically. As the creature started to roll over on its side, Asha screamed out, "Jump!" They all jumped out together before the creature tried to roll onto its back and crush them.

"It's an enormous snake!" Asha said, thinking to herself, *nothing can surprise me anymore!* The snake heard her voice and turned around to come after them.

"Run," she shouted.

Asha, Najeena and Spirit started to run as fast as they could toward the mountains. The owl went after the snake and clawed at its eyes, so that it couldn't see them anymore. There was a loud shriek that made Asha stop running and turn around to see what was happening. The owl had scratched the eyes of this monstrous snake and blinded it, but it was still trying to pursue them.

"It can smell us, we must defeat it!" Asha shouted out, but she didn't know how to. This giant serpent seemed just too powerful. As the snake got to her, she started to panic. She looked all around to see if she could find something that could help. The owl flew over to Asha and grabbed the peacock feather out of her necklace. The feather stabbed Asha in the arm and drew her blood onto its sharp point.

"Ouch, what was that for?" Asha asked angrily. The owl put the feather back into Asha's hand and looked toward the snake. "You want me to stab the snake with this feather?" she asked, very confused. "Seriously?"

The snake was slithering closer, and Asha had no other choice; it was do or die. She ran as fast as she could toward the serpent, jumped on top of the monstrous snake and stabbed it in between its eyes. The snake screeched so loudly that it hurt Asha's ears and made her fall off. Spirit came galloping over and she jumped onto his back. They ran away from the snake as quickly as they could.

As they got closer to the mountains, they turned around to look at the snake. It was finally dead and they were satisfied that they could safely carry on their journey to the ocean.

It was a beautiful afternoon and the countryside was green and full of flowers. Asha knew that they had to be close, as they passed in between the grassy mountains.

"I think we are nearly there. I can smell the salt from the ocean," Asha said excitedly.

They finally made it through the grassy hills. On the other side, there was a gorgeous town with paved roads and golden temples.

This was the most picturesque part of Gujarat, which felt very modern to Asha. It made her kingdom of

Panchala seem ancient in comparison. It was as beautiful as the golden palace that the handsome prince lived in. The people of the city all seemed so happy while they were selling their goods, completely oblivious of what was about to happen if Asha was to succeed. If all went to plan, there would be an island city that was thousands of years old appearing right off their coast!

Will everyone just start to remember their gods and goddesses, where we came from, and how our greed, lust and selfishness has doomed us to the world we live in today? Asha was thinking to herself. *Will the evil just disappear when our consciousness awakens?* She had so many unanswered questions.

Asha saw a beautiful temple that seemed to be calling out to her. She stopped outside, stared at it for a while and then decided to go in. As she walked up the stairs, Asha started to get an overwhelming feeling inside of her, a feeling of comfort and love, like a doting mother's warm arms wrapped around her. It felt as though she was home, even though she had never been here before.

As Asha walked through the large wooden doors, she saw a handsome statue of Krishna, but this time with a ravishing woman.

"Was this his goddess wife?" she thought out loud.

"Yes, that is the Goddess Lakshmi. Lakshmi came to earth as the incarnation of Rukmini," a voice said from behind her. Asha turned around to see who it was.

There standing behind her was a guru, an old man with long gray hair and beard, dressed in a long gold robe.

"I'm sorry to have startled you, Princess Asha," the guru said.

"You know who I am?"

"Of course I do, Your Highness. We have been waiting for this day ever since you were born," he replied.

"Why don't my parents know about my destiny, the reason for me to be alive, if so many other people know?" she asked.

"They knew, Your Highness, but your journey needed to be pure and your mind untouched. It had to be all you with no outside influences. We are all given the choice of free will. We can choose the dark path or the enlightened path," he preached.

"But if it's my destiny, then how do I have a choice?" Asha asked.

"Destinies can change, Asha, we can change them and that is a part of the journey. Some choose the wrong path, and some choose the right one. There are others that just don't know which way to go, which leaves them living a very uncertain life: kind of like living in chaos, like always having the feeling that you needed to do something, but you can't quite remember what it was."

Asha stood up, and the guru stood up with her and walked her to the doors. When Asha went outside, it was starting to get dark. The magnificent blue supermoon was shining brightly over the ocean.

"I suppose I should go to the ocean-side and complete my destiny," Asha said, flashing a smile at the guru.

"Good luck my child. I will keep you in my thoughts," he said and gave a little bow with his hands clasped together. Asha bowed back at him and headed down the stairs to her horse. Najeena was taking a drink at one of the many water stations and the owl was sitting on the brick wall, waiting patiently.

"It is time," she said to all of the animals. The owl looked at her with big yellow eyes, stood up tall and nodded. They all headed off to the ocean side to call upon the Sea God.

Chapter 10 - The Sea God

The waves were gently splashing against the rocks and the sun had completely set. It was just the bright supermoon and the four travelers sitting on the ocean's edge. Asha started to feel nervous that she wouldn't be able to complete this mission and that everyone would be disappointed in her.

"What will happen to our world if I don't succeed?" she asked herself out loud. "Will my people become lost? Will we all be our own doom and gloom?" It was a very scary thought for the princess. After all that she had seen in the past weeks of her journey, she couldn't imagine all of that evil taking over the world.

The princess took the sacred water out of her bag and drank some of it. Then she poured the rest into the ocean. Asha reached for her bag and opened the box with the flute inside.

This is it, show time! There is no turning back now. She thought. Asha removed the flute from the box, took a few deep breaths and put the flute to her lips. She blew into it, but again no music came out. She tried again and again and again.

"This is useless!" she shouted out.

"They must all have it wrong. How am I the chosen one? I can't even play this flute." Asha was just about to throw the flute into the ocean out of frustration when the owl grabbed a hold of it and took it out of her hands. She flew in front of her and started fiercely spinning in the air. Asha could see the owl glowing brightly, like the sun shining brightly in your eyes on a sunny day. Within a few seconds, the owl had transformed and the beautiful goddess Lakshmi was floating in the air in front of her.

"You must have faith in yourself, my dear child," the goddess softly said.

"You doubt yourself, so the music cannot be heard. Close your eyes and listen, the music is all around us, not just in this flute. You have to listen with your heart and then you will hear the song."

Asha was stunned that her travelling companion was apparently a deity!

"All I want to do is fulfill my destiny and change the world for the better," Asha said with a tear running down her cheek.

"None of us can change the whole world, Asha. No one is expecting that of you," said Lakshmi. "The change has to start within ourselves, within you. Once your consciousness is awakened, it will then encourage others to also make that change. Imagine a world without ego, greed and selfishness!" Lakshmi said as she handed Asha the flute.

"Believe in who you are and in all the good around you, then you will hear the music. Trust in all the decency that is in your heart." The goddess faded away.

Asha looked all around to see if she had turned back into the owl, but she had not. It was just Asha, Spirit and Najeena now.

"Would anybody else like to reveal that they can actually talk to me please?" Asha said to the animals. Najeena let out a gentle moo and Spirit nuzzled up to Asha, nudging the flute to her lips.

Asha put the flute to her mouth once again, but this time closed her eyes and meditated on everything and everyone she loved with all her heart.

As she put her lips to the flute and blew air into it, she could hear the most magical music. It was so beautiful that the waves started to move with the sounds of the tune. Asha opened her eyes and looked out to the ocean, where a huge whirlpool had started to form. The ocean waves became so forceful that Asha had to stand up and step back from the edge in case it tried to pull her in. Spirit started to rear up in fear of this large whirlpool sucking everything around into its center.

A few moments later, a giant half-man and half-fish arose out of the vortex. He had a long gray beard and hair. He was very muscular and wore large gold cuff bracelets on his wrists with every shade of blue jewel set inside of them. It was only his torso that Asha could see; the rest of his body was within the water. She could see just the top of the scales that wrapped around his waist in colors of dark blue and aqua. As he came closer to Asha, he seemed even larger in stature.

"Well done Princess Asha," he said with his deep, godly voice. "You truly are pure of heart and mind to be able to summon me."

Asha bowed down to the Sea God and then asked, "My Lord, I have come to ask you to please raise Dwarka again." They stared at each other for a moment, and then she continued, "Our world is starting to fall apart. No one has faith or belief anymore. It seems that humans have forgotten where we came from and who we truly are."

"If I were to raise Dwarka again, how can you be sure mankind will change for the good?" he asked. "It was the greed and selfishness of humanity that brought this beautiful city down to the ocean floor," he continued, without allowing Asha to answer the question.

"Humans have forgotten about our past because nobody speaks of it. We cannot believe or understand something that we have never been taught. To most of mankind, gods, goddesses, and Dwarka are all a myth," Asha said firmly and confidently.

"Asha, you must understand that seeing isn't believing; believing is seeing. There are many things that stand right in front of you, but if you choose not to believe in them, then they do not exist for you. All living creatures have a conscience that is within them, that speaks to them, but some just choose to ignore it. Do you understand, my child?"

"With all due respect, my lord, how can we change the future if we don't understand who we truly are or where we came from, or why we are even here?" Asha questioned.

"Asha, your purity and optimism have me convinced. I will raise Dwarka for the future of humanity. However, you need to fully understand that this is not the end of your journey, or even mankind's journey; this is only the beginning. There is still much to be done if you want to save mankind for the better and there will be serious consequences if change isn't made."

"What do you mean this isn't the end? What else has to be done?" Asha asked, feeling very anxious.

"You will know when the time is right, princess. I must warn you that if all fails, this world of yours will be doomed, the darkness will take over and there will be no turning back." The Sea God slowly submerged into the ocean depths and all went very still. The violent whirlpool subsided.

Asha was feeling very confused and uncertain.

What was the Sea God talking about? What else was there for her to do? Why hadn't he raised Dwarka like he said he was going to?

Asha turned around and was about to walk back onto the ornately paved road when the ground started to shake. It felt like a huge earthquake running through Gujarat. She could hear screams from the city people running out of their homes to protect themselves from being hit by anything falling down. It was a scene of total chaos!

The water started to rise and the tremors got worse. Spirit took off in terror and Najeena looked at Asha with fear all over her little face.

"Run, Najeena, run away as fast as you can," shouted Asha, but Najeena refused to leave her side.

Large rocks started to rise from the ocean floor, and waves started to crash up onto the mainland, knocking Asha and Najeena over. Asha tried to get up and run, but another wave came over and knocked her down. This time it was so strong that it threw them into a wall across the pavement, and knocked the princess unconscious. Najeena was nowhere to be found; the waves had taken her too.

Moments later, everything went really quiet. The ocean calmed down and the tremors went away almost as quickly as they had arisen. By the light of the supermoon, a beautiful island city with streams and waterfalls and beautiful flowers and green grass had emerged. The buildings were big and beautiful with gold trimming.

Dwarka the Golden City had risen!

Chapter 11 - Beginning of the End

It was dark and there were lots of voices and chattering around Asha. That was what she heard as she was drifting in and out of consciousness. The princess lay there with an aching head on the pavement, trying to open her eyes.

"Princess Asha, can you hear me?" said a familiar voice. "Princess Asha, please wake up."

Asha slowly opened her eyes. The sun was about to rise and there were many people hovering around. The princess had been unconscious for most of the night, and had missed the entire spectacle of Dwarka rising out of the ocean.

"Please, give the princess some space," the familiar voice said. As Asha started to regain her sight, she could see a blurred vision of a handsome young man. It was the prince of Gujarat. "Princess Asha, are you okay? Can you move?" he asked.

"I think so," she said, trying to get up, but Asha fell back down from the dizziness.

"Easy, don't try to stand, we will help you. Bring me some water," the prince ordered one of his royal guards. "Here, drink some water, it will help you." Asha took a sip and tried to rise again. This time she got up a little farther but fell to the side into the prince's arms. "It's okay, take your time, I've got you," he said as they gazed into each other's eyes.

"What happened?" she asked weakly.

"You did it Asha, you raised Dwarka," the prince replied. "Our people will now begin to question the history of mankind. The lies that they have been told will now be questioned and the true stories can be taught. We can now teach our children about who we truly are and bring back the good in this world," he continued.

"I want to see Dwarka. I need to see it," Asha said, trying to stand up again.

"I will take you there, but you need to rest first. Let my guards take you back to the palace. We will have a healer come and look at you, and then I will take you to Dwarka. I promise," the prince said as he and his guards lifted Asha to her feet and carried her away.

Asha looked behind her to see if she could make out Dwarka, but all she could see were hundreds of people standing around, looking and pointing at the beautiful golden island.

"Wait!" Asha shouted. "Where is Najeena?"

"She is safe, Asha, one of the guards has taken her back to the palace," the prince assured her.

Asha lay on the bed while the healer checked her for injuries.

"You have quite a bump on the back of your head, Your Highness," he said. "You must rest to avoid symptoms of a shock."

"Thank you, we will make sure she rests," the prince said to the healer while standing by the door.

"Make sure you do, sire, or she will take much longer to heal. She was very lucky, it could have been much worse," the healer said as he packed his equipment into his bag. He turned around, looked at Asha, and said, "If you need me, you know where to find me." He bowed to the prince before walking out of the room.

"Now that he is gone, let's go and see Dwarka," Asha said, climbing out of bed.

"I don't think so," the prince said as he tucked her back in. "Dwarka isn't going anywhere, and you need to rest. I will take you there in the morning."

"Ugh, this is very frustrating and unfair," Asha said, folding her arms in a huff.

"Get some rest, and I will take you to see Dwarka in the morning," the prince said again as he kissed her forehead and left her room for the night.

The next morning Asha woke up bright and early, hurriedly dressed and was ready to go before the prince came to escort her. As the prince went to knock, Asha flung both doors wide open, nearly knocking him down.

"Your Highness, I'm so sorry. Are you okay?" Asha asked, embarrassed.

"It's okay, I don't need my nose," he said jokingly. "I guess you are feeling better and ready to go." He grinned. "We will ride there. My guards found your horse. He is saddled up and ready for you to ride. If you are feeling up to it?"

"Yes, I'm most definitely ready to go," the princess said excitedly as she rushed down the hallway.

They both mounted their horses and headed for the city. When they arrived, the prince had arranged for a boat to be at the dock, waiting to take them over to the island.

They left their horses with the royal guards and got onto the boat. A sailor rowed them over to the island city.

The men tied the boat up to one of the docks and helped the princess onto the island. Asha's heart was racing. She did not know what to expect when she reached Dwarka.

"Are you ready to look around?" the prince asked. "It's a big city, so we have a lot of walking to do."

Asha took in several deep breaths and nodded her head. They headed for the waterfalls first. It was so beautiful: the flowers, the waterfalls and the big trees. Asha could visualize Krishna playing his flute with his people dancing around him. It all felt so surreal that Asha had to pinch herself to make sure that this was all really happening.

"It's so wonderful. It's better than I ever imagined it would be," Asha said to the prince, sniffing the flowers. "It just seems too good to be real. I can actually feel the presence of the people that once lived here. They were all so happy, and they had everything. Why would people destroy that?" Asha asked sadly.

"They wanted more, they became greedy and selfish. They forgot who they were and why they were there in the first place," the prince said. "Now, thanks to you, we can learn from our ancestors' mistakes and rebuild a better future for our children."

Asha smiled modestly at the prince, knowing that it was because of her that the world had another chance. She didn't need or want any recognition; she was much too humble for that. "Thank you for the praise, but it was my duty to do this. I want peace in our world just as much as the next person." Asha took his hand and headed for the center of the city.

After an hour of walking, they finally reached the city center, where the buildings were old and fascinating.

There was gold trim that glistened in the sun around the edges of each building. The two of them could only imagine how amazing it would have been to live there during the reign of Krishna. It was the era when gods and humans coexisted, a time where everything must have felt magical.

The sun was setting quickly, so they decided to head back to the boat before it got too dark. As they were crossing the ocean, it occurred to Asha that the flute was missing. The prince could see the concern in her face and asked her, "What is wrong? You look upset."

"It's the flute, I don't know where it's gone," she answered. "The last time I had it was when I summoned the Sea God."

"Maybe it's in the ocean with the Sea God. I wouldn't worry too much. If it's ever needed again, I'm sure it will resurface," the prince said reassuringly.

"Let's go home, and I will ride back to your palace with you in the morning. I'm sure that your parents are missing you."

The next morning after breakfast, the prince and Asha said their goodbyes to the king and queen of Gujarat. They headed on their horses with Najeena and royal guards over the hills toward the Himalayas. It was the perfect day for a new beginning for Princess Asha.

After a long journey back to the Himalayas, they finally reached Panchala. Asha's parents were standing on the grand staircase outside watching the horses come through the gates. The queen was stretching her neck to see if she could see the princess. As Asha rode in on Spirit, the queen ran down the stairs and pulled Asha off of her horse before she could dismount, and hugged her tightly in her arms. The King ran down and joined the queen and Asha in the reunion.

"It's so good to be home," Asha said looking up at her parents.

Epilogue

Back in Dwarka, a greedy old man in a boat saw an object glistening in the sunlight at the bottom of the ocean. Wondering what it was, he decided to jump into the water and dive down to get this shiny relic that had caught his eye. The old man grabbed it, climbed back into his boat, and grinned evilly, knowing the immense value of what he had just found.

"I know who would pay a lot of gold for this," the greedy old man said and cackled as he rowed his boat toward the sunset..........................

--- THE END ---

www.ingramcontent.com/pod-product-compliance
Lightning Source LLC
Chambersburg PA
CBHW072227190626
46809CB00017B/1241

9781999602024